MINDO

CHASED BY THE DRAGONS

EVA WILDER

ALYSE ZAFTIG

EVA WILDER

eISBN: 978-1-63481-008-1

ISBN: 9798686343931

My gaze bounced between the two of them. Alonso had his hair tousled, and he was leaning back on his chair. Victor had perfect posture, and his hair was gelled perfectly. Both of them could have featured on the cover of a magazine. *Vegas.*

"Yes."

Alonso was on top of me almost before I got to the end of the word. He took my hands in his big ones and pinned them to the back of the couch. He gently bit my neck before parting my lips with his tongue and kissing me deeply.

Victor wanted to get in on this action, too. I could feel Alonso being pushed to one side, as Victor put his huge hand inside of my top. He pinched my nipple, and I jerked. His other hand went to unbutton my jeans, and he had to use two hands to get the button open. I was really self conscious about the pudge that formed when I sat down, and I tried to back away, even though there was no room. Lifting my shirt, Victor went down to kiss my stomach.

RETURNING TO ECUADOR

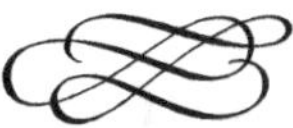

I was exhausted. After I went back to Rochester to attend my uncle's funeral, I'd had to stay at my aunt's house. I wasn't going to home to my mom. My aunt had a good relationship with me, but she was grieving. It was a downer to listen to her cry at night. She wouldn't get out of bed.

I hadn't been particularly close to my uncle, but I was close to my aunt, an island of sanity in the chaos that was my childhood. I made sure that the dishes were done, the floors were vacuumed, and the laundry was done. I sent thank you notes for all of the condolence letters that she received. I couldn't lift the burden of losing someone my aunt loved, but I could take care of the little stuff so that she didn't have to.

I was home for only a week, thank goodness. It was depressing to be around my aunt, who was normally a pretty little ray of sunshine. I flew back to Ecuador on Saturday night to resume my life, one that didn't involve sending a million thank you notes. The biggest problems in my Ecuadorian life were huge essays written in Spanish. Even though I was conversationally fluent, anglicisms always slipped out when I was writing. Essays in Spanish like a mosquito bite versus a third-degree burn.

While I was gone, Esther had all of my professors email me Powerpoints of the lectures that I'd missed. Because of my bereavement, they gave me an extra week to finish all of my assignments. I knew that I'd fall further behind if I actually lollygagged, so I did them all on the Sunday that I got back, no matter how exhausted I was from flying from NYC to Quito on Saturday.

My host family was very quiet. They worked, they bought food from restaurants, and we ate dinner in silence every night. That might not have been an ideal situation for another person, but it suited me. They didn't mind if I went out late at night with my friends, mostly Alice, and I didn't mind that they left me alone and basically only fed me. With the Internet and my laptop, I could be pretty happy wherever I was. When I came in at night, I was quiet and courteous to them. It was a dynamic that worked, and frankly one much better than the home I'd grown up in.

I texted Alice on Sunday night.

Done with homework. Should we go to the bars?

Can't. Rafael Correa passed a law saying that you can't buy alcohol on Sundays at this time of night.

Ugh. I'd forgotten.

Can I come over, then?

Yes. I'll tell my mom.

Alice lived in the apartment below me, which definitely helped cement our friendship. We went to school together on the same bus, and sometimes we shared a taxi. It literally cost a dollar to get from our apartment building at El Telegrafo and Avenida de los Shyris to go to school. It had weirded me out at first that there were no absolute locations in Ecuador, but I'd gotten used to being told that places existed at intersections after a few months.

I took my phone, put on my shoes, and went down the stairs.

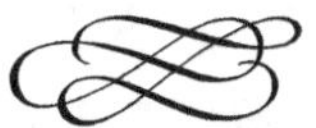

Alice already had it open and was waiting for me.

"Hey."

"Hey. How was your trip?"

"Sad." I shrugged.

"I can't believe you went through all your homework in one day, Gab."

"I had to. You know me. I can't stand leaving things undone."

Alice laughed. "I guess that's true. Come on. I'll make us some smoothies.

Do you want watermelon or guanabana?"

"I can get watermelon smoothies at home. Let's make guanabana today." I'd never eaten guanabana before getting to Ecuador, but I'd quickly fallen in love with the taste. It was the perfect thing for a night when I couldn't go out and party with my friends. We were pretty tame, as far as partying went, but we had a lot of fun in La Mariscal at trivia nights. We went to Finn McCool's on Tuesdays and the South American Explorer's Club on Wednesdays. It was wonderful — nerdy, yes, but wonderful. Where else could you get free drinks for being smart?

La Mariscal was also known as Gringolandia, for a good reason. Most of the people in the district were white, and it was really a playground for them. The pubs charged gringo prices, which were twice to three times what normal restaurants charged, but the waiters and waitresses always spoke fluent English. I'd gone to Sports Planet for the Super Bowl, which I don't even watch when I'm in the United States. I found hundreds of homesick Americans eating nachos and hamburgers while watching large men rough each other up while fighting over the pigskin. There's something quintessentially American about beating up one another for a few seconds, and then both sides taking a breather.

On nights like tonight, when there was no alcohol, it was a dead zone. It wouldn't take me out of my head, still spinning from the rude shock of going home for my uncle's funeral. If I were home, I'd make smores on a night like tonight. Although Ecuador had chocolate in abundance, finding graham crackers and marshmallows were a little more difficult. I'd never thought of how important small comforts were until I went to a country that didn't have them.

Thank goodness for alcohol, which was universal in human civilization. Alice took a little bit of the host family's stash to spike our smoothies, and we took them into her room. We put them on her nightstand. Alice put on Pandora, and I sat with my back against the bed while she surfed around on her laptop.

"It was exhausting."

"Yeah?"

"I don't know. I'm not really good with grief. It changes people."

"Yeah, I'm sure it does."

I was quiet for a while. "I think that if I died, no one would really miss me."

"I'd miss you. I'm sure there are a lot of friends and family who would miss you. You'd be surprised by how many lives yours touches."

"I think that it would be a shock, sure, but I don't really think that anybody would miss me after. My mom definitely wouldn't, and my aunt's in her own world now, after her husband's death."

"What about your friends?"

"I don't really keep in touch. And really, you're the best fit I've ever had with another person. You know when to be quiet and when to talk, which is hard to find."

"Thanks, sugar." She gave me a hug from the bed, which could also be construed as a chokehold in other circumstances. "Is that ok with you? Do you want to change that?"

I didn't know. "I feel like there should be more to my life. I'm an honors student. I have a job. I do my homework. I have two majors, because I enjoy both Spanish and Psychology."

"You're a really impressive person."

"I'm not, really. I'm just getting by."

"That's how everyone feels. We're all just getting by."

I bent my legs, and I rested my chin on my knees. "I guess. I just feel like there should be something more, you know? Everyone when I was growing up told me that I was so special, so smart, so good at everything. And then when I got to college, the professors demanded more and more. I was in honors classes, and there wasn't a lot of positive reinforcement. I don't feel special anymore. I feel pretty average."

Alice laughed. "Welcome to real life, Gab. The definition of average is that most people are. You're a psych major. You know that."

"I guess." I looked down at the floor. "I just wish that there was a way for me to have a bigger impact, I suppose. It's like I've come into this world, and I'm going to leave it without any kind of footprint. I'll just die a quiet death and not leave any kind of muss behind. I don't even have a cat or fish that would miss me."

Alice slid on the floor next to me, and she put her head on my shoulder. "People would miss you."

"I want to do something. I want to

be someone who does something meaningful, something that means something to a lot of people."

"You'll find it. You'll find the right place, and then it'll seem so easy and natural for you to have a high impact. I'm sure of it." She gave me a side hug, and then she went back up on her bed.

"That's seriously enough of me being maudlin. How about you? How has the last week been for you?"

"Good, I guess. I got lost in the Galapagos for a while."

BLACK HUMOR

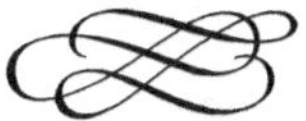

I sprang up. *"What?"*

She shrugged. "It wasn't a big deal. I got lost while snorkeling on Floreana, but Esther sent out a search party to find me. They found me in perfect condition. They made me see a doctor on Isabela, and he said I wasn't even dehydrated, which I should've been from swimming in the sea water."

"Jeez, Alice. That's so scary. Are you ok?"

"Yeah, I'm fine. What was annoying was that Esther wouldn't let me out of her sight after that. I also had to deal with Catie." She rolled her eyes.

"Catie's such a nice girl. It's just that…"

"She doesn't know when to stop? Yeah." Alice rolled to her back to stare at the ceiling. "Your uncle was so inconsiderate, dying when *I* needed you." She was such a queen sometimes.

I laughed. Alice's brand of humor was just like my own. And yeah, it was black humor, but it made me feel better. "I'll be sure to tell him when I see him next."

"Well, whichever of us sees him first can tell him."

"Deal." I reached up to drink some

of my rum smoothie. "Did you get any good pictures?"

"Nah, I didn't think it was worth the hassle. Catie has that waterproof camera, though, and she posted a million pictures of the Galapagos on her Facebook. You want to look?"

"Totally."

I got up and sat on her bed. She pulled up Catie's photo albums on Facebook, and we went through them together.

"You missed the part where we swam with penguins."

"Shut up. You did not."

"We totally did. There are really tiny penguins on Isabela, and they're the northernmost penguins ever. They are the only ones to cross the Equator, which runs through Isabela."

"No way!"

"Yeah, they swim on the cold side, which is furnished with water from the Humboldt Current which runs along the side of Chile."

"I can't believe I missed that!" I wailed. "Could there be anything cooler?"

"You missed the wild dolphins, too, but you can swim with dolphins anytime at Sea World."

"True."

I saw a million sea lion pictures. One was of a sea lion just hanging out on a metal slide on a children's playground. It was hilarious. There were tons of pictures of the water and of the sky. I'd missed parts where they'd gone through museums, but after a while, all of the Galapagos starts to look the same.

"I'm pretty much done." Alice nodded, and then she closed her laptop. "Do you want to play Bananagrams?"

"Yeah!"

Bananagrams with two people was way more intense than Bananagrams with an officially sanctioned number of people. We were both pretty good with finding new words, and we could beat each other pretty equally. Bananagrams was our thing, alongside no-stakes poker played with candy.

She got out the yellow Bananagrams bag, and we sat on the floor and played until her host mom called us for a late dinner. Her mom made chicken soup with mote, fried yuca with pan-seared Chilean sea bass, and banana cake for dinner. Everything tasted great. I'd noticed that the flavors were stronger in Ecuador than in the United States. Her mom was a better cook than their maid.

Their maid came during the day. She did all of the housecleaning, cooked lunch, did the laundry, and shopped for groceries. In America, it was the purview of the ultra-wealthy to have household help. In Ecuador, it was part of being middle class. The minimum wage per month in Ecuador was around $200 a month. If household help in the United States cost that much, a lot more people would have maids.

So, after dinner, cleanup was trivially easy. We collected all the plates and put them in the kitchen sink for the maid to clean the next morning. I was too used to the luxury of having someone take care of me. In college, I had to cook my own Easy Mac and take out my own trash.

Alice and I went back to her room.

"I know what will make you feel better."

"What?"

"A Taylor Swift dance party!"

I smiled. It was so ridiculous, but it was true. The wonderful thing about Taylor Swift's music was that it had a couple layers. There was the surface layer, the one that fools you with the happy beats. It made you think that she was singing pop. But at the heart of each song was some kind of despair, the kind that had made Taylor's career in country. That's what I loved the most. The desperation in Style wasn't evident when you just listened to it. Everyone thought that the music video was really weird, with the broken mirrors and all the imagery, but it was the best representation of what the song actually meant. If you took away the electronic dance music beat, the songs were just as sad as the country she'd had on earlier albums, like White Horse, Back to December, and Begin Again. The black despair that was worthy of Evanescence was what brought me back every time.

Alice put on *1989*, and we spent the next half hour and change singing along with the lyrics and dancing around like fools in her room. The rum hadn't hurt any, and it gave me a good sense of wellbeing, which was helped by Alice knowing the perfect way to cheer me up. I knew that it's weird that sadness and despair underlying a happy tune cheered me up, but it did. It reminded me of the Glass

Menagerie by Tennessee Williams. He'd written a play, not a musical, and his idea of the underlying theme song was something that sounded like circus music but had the bitter taste of despair. That's what Taylor Swift's music sounded like to me.

I was sweaty and out of breath by the end. Alice had done a great job of getting me out of my head, but it was late. We had school tomorrow.

"I should go. I'll be by tomorrow morning to grab you so we can go to school."

"Later, girl." Alice walked me out. I climbed the stairs to my penthouse apartment. It sounded more luxurious than it really was. In a developing country, the penthouse was simply the highest level in a building without an elevator or air conditioning.

PLANNING

The school week passed pretty uneventfully. I caught up with all of my professors, and I turned in all of my assignments. They made soothing noises about my uncle dying. I accepted their condolences, but it was almost meaningless to me. I wasn't close to him; it was only important because of my aunt.

On Thursday, Alice came up to me

while I was in the computer lab checking Facebook between classes.

"Hey."

"What's up?"

"Some of us want to go to Mindo again. Do you want to come with us?"

I thought about it. The only thing that would be there for me this weekend was a lot of empty time. "I'll come."

"Great! We can go tubing and zi-plining again."

I groaned. "You know that I'm too short to fit in the tubes properly. They don't carry child-sized tubes."

"You were fine. It's fine. You just hold the handles the whole time. You don't need to be supported by your feet."

I raised my eyebrows at her.

"It'll be fine. You can swim, right?"

"Whatever. I'm in. You know how Marta told us last time that there's a three-day pass for ziplining?"

"Yeah."

"I think that we should do that, if we're going back to Mindo."

"Do you want to book all of our activities through her?"

"Why not? It's the same price, and she has the phone numbers of everything in town."

Alice snorted. "It's not a town. It's a wee village in the clouds."

"That you got lost in."

Alice blushed, although you'd think that she would be used to being teased about that before. The first time that we went to Mindo, she kept getting lost. I loved her. She was my best friend. However, she had the worst sense of direction I'd ever seen in a functioning human being.

"*Anyways,* as I was saying, we can just go to Casa de Celia again. You and I can share a private room, and the rest of the girls can go to that cool treehouse room that they have."

"Sounds good to me. Are you making the arrangements?"

She looked at me with a plea in her eyes. "I was actually hoping you would."

I sighed internally. I got a reputation in the group for being an ultra-planner, just because I actually checked where we were going before we leapt. I preferred to take the bus rapid transit lines, the Ecovia, Trolebus, and Metrobus, anywhere we could possibly go without a taxi. After having the excrement scared out of me by the head of diplomatic security at the US Embassy in Quito during the orientation I'd had within the first few days, I knew all about taxi secuestro. Taxi drivers would kidnap people and dose them with scopolamine, which inhibited memory formation and made them acquiescent. We'd been in a lot of taxis since coming to Ecuador, but I preferred to be safer than sorry. It had earned me a reputation of being the cautious one. It was a habit that had gotten me the nickname Tantor when I was kid. I still couldn't watch Tarzan.

"Fine."

Alice beamed. "I'll tell them." I thought that she hadn't actually thought it was a question. I needed to loosen up and not be the one who de facto handled all the details. I was always the guidebook. I needed to take more risks. It was hard, though, because careful planning was how I'd survived my childhood. Every time my mom went to the grocery store, I quietly took some of the nonperishable items and kept them in my room. Who knew when she'd go again? She wasn't a reliable person, and I was.

I'd been so jealous as a kid, watching other kids go to Dad's Club soccer and Brownies. Mom didn't care enough to take the time to take me to any activities. The late bus in middle school had been the only reason I'd gotten to join the soccer team. The money to buy cleats and all my other gear came from my aunt. As soon as I was 14, I went through the process to get a work permit, so I'd have my own money. I waitressed every hour I could

at the local Buffalo Wild Wings. I'd
had to quit the soccer team to work as
much as I did, but I still refereed kids'
soccer games on the weekends during
the days when there wasn't a big game.
My manager was in college, and she
was wonderful and respectful of my
need to go to school and also referee
soccer. She let me pick up all the hours
I could possibly take while having
time for other things in my life. I'd
made my way up to assistant manager
at BWW, and I'd been able to transfer
to the BWW in my college town. I'd
been working there for a long time.

It was really weird for me to not
have that constant in my life, the late
hours, the rude customers, the regulars,
my coworkers. I volunteered on Tuesdays and Thursdays at an organization,
Ciclopolis, that focused on promoting

bicycling, which had been my primary transportation for a very long time. In a crowded little capital city located in a plateau with mountains trapping in all the pollution, bicycling was the sanest way for to people get around. Instead of a mass conversion to bicycling, though, they had instituted pico y plata, which did not reduce emissions. It just meant that you were obligated to take a taxi to and from work one day of the week. The taxi drivers were happy about it, but none of the rest of the Quito natives were.

My volunteer work at Ciclopolis had provided my spending money. There was a special scholarship for people who went to a handful of developing countries who stated an intent to volunteer. Other people in college sneered at the idea of volun-tourism, but I really liked the concept. It was a way to get immersed in the community, and you could meet people outside of the halls of academia.

Everyone else had Tuesday and Thursday classes. All of us went out of town on Fridays together, or we all stayed in town together. It was always one or the other. Even if a group of us broke off, like the group of the five of us going to Mindo, there'd be another group going to Atacames or Mon-tanita. It got complicated with a larger group, so I was glad to have a group small enough that you could count it on one hand.

I called up Marta.

"Hello, Marta. How's it going?"

"Well. And you, Gabriella? You are well?"

"Yes, I am. My friends and I are planning on coming to your hostel again. We were wondering if we could make reservations for the five of us. We'd like your treehouse and the little front room you have."

"Ah, let me check to see if they are free." I heard the sound of pages turning. "Yes, we have not yet booked them. You may have them. Would you like anything else?"

"Yes, you did an excellent job last time of setting up all of our activities. Could you set up tubing passes for one day and ziplining for two days?"

"You are staying 2 nights?"

"Yes."

"You have already been tubing and ziplining, I know."

"Yes."

"Would you like something new? Are any of you early risers?"

"I can be. Why?"

"There's an ecological station with German scientists who will show you around the cloud forest for about $40 per group."

"Is it worth it? Is it a good tour?"

"Yes, it's very beautiful. You'll see everything that makes the Andean cloud forest so special."

"Ok, we'll book that, too. Could you split that cost 5 ways when you set up our tab?"

"Yes."

"We'll give you a down payment when we get there on Friday morning on the earliest bus."

"Ok, I will have everything ready for you then."

"Thanks, Marta."

"You are welcome. I look forward to seeing you and your friends."

I went into our classroom. I nudged Alice. "Done."

"You're a star." She beamed. "That was so fast. You're our travel agent."

"You could pay me…" I teased.

"We'll pay you in batidos." It was the currency of choice for our group. With fresh food so cheap in Ecuador, we ate luxurious three-course meals for $2.50. All of us were obsessed with batidos, and we sought them out wherever we were. When we made bets, they were for batidos. We gave each other IOUs that we often lost, but it was fun.

"Deal. Who is coming, anyway?"

"It's you and me, obviously. Then, Fitz, Catie, and Jade."

I made a face.

"Catie's going to be in the tree-house. You know that she's nice."

I sighed. "I guess."

"Anyways, pack your swimsuit and hiking shoes. You know that ziplining is a huge climb."

"Will do."

Our anthropology professor began the Powerpoint, and we shut up.

BUS RIDE

On Friday morning, Alice and I met heinously early in the morning. I force-fed her coffee, because she was always a zombie in the morning. I needed us to move quickly. With all of our gear, it would take a long time to walk to the nearest Metrobus station. I hailed a cab, and we had it take us there.

We took the Metrobus up to La Ofelia, the northern bus station. Most of the time, we traveled out of Quitumbe, the southern bus station that was connected to the Ecovia. La Ofelia was only for Atacames and Mindo.

Fitz, Jade, and Catie were there already, raiding a vending machine for candy bars for breakfast. They'd already bought their bus tickets, so Alice and I went to get two more tickets. While Alice and I were in line, Fitz, Jade, and Catie stowed their luggage in the bus, and then they boarded. After waiting for 10 people, we finally got to the window. They gave us a ticket, a boleto, and sent us on our way. Alice and I shoved our stuff under the bus in the compartments, and then we climbed up the stairs to join our friends.

Fitz and Jade were already dozing

quietly in their seats. Catie was wide awake and bushy-tailed.

"Hey, guys!"

It was a mistake to drink that coffee. I didn't have to look at Alice to see her rolling her eyes.

"Hey, girl. Alice and I are pretty wiped, so we're probably going to sleep like Fitz and Jade."

"Oh, yeah, ok. I'll just read *No Se Lo Digas a Nadie*, then." We all had to read it for our contemporary Andean literature class. It was a horrifying and semi-autobiographical account of being homosexual while part of the upper crust of Peru. Part of the Latin American culture was a concept called machismo, where guys had to be as macho as possible. The American cult of masculinity was a comparable concept. Homosexuality was the complete opposite of alpha machismo, and it was frowned upon and shameful. His dad was a caricature of machismo embodied, while his mother was the softer feminine side who loved him and would do anything for him.

My host mom, when she saw the book, got upset that I was reading it.

Why are you reading this trash?

It's for literature class.

How dare they? You came all the way from the United States, and they give you Jaime Bayly!

That, of course, spurred me to read the entirety far before I had to. I was quietly sick of the homophobia rampant in Latin America, and it was an act of defiance to read a book that had scandalized the Peruvian elite and my host mom.

"It's so long," Alice moaned. It was

over 400 pages in our non-native language.

"That's why it's ideal!" chirped Catie.

"Have fun." I settled into my seat, balled up my jacket, and pretended to sleep. I felt Alice lean on my shoulder, and despite the caffeine, I was actually asleep within minutes.

ARRIVING

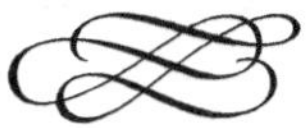

I could feel someone shaking my shoulder.

"Hey, guys! Wake up! Wake up!"

Catie was worse than an alarm clock.

"I'm up. I'm up." *Please stop shaking me, thanks.* I opened my eyes. Alice was blearily rubbing her eyes, and I could see Fitz and Jade yawning and stretching out.

Catie was bouncing up and down in the bus aisle. "Let's go, guys!"

It is too early for this.

I touched Alice's shoulder. "Move it, slowpoke."

"I'm going, I'm going." She yawned. "Tired."

"We all are. Get your A into G, girl."

Catie lead our half-asleep group down the steps, and we walked to Casa de Celia. Mindo was extremely small. There was a central plaza that was formed by four streets, two sets of parallel lines that crossed each other. It formed a tic-tac-toe board, and Casa de Celia wasn't far from the bus station.

"Hello, girls! How happy I am to see your beautiful faces!" Marta gave all of us a kiss on the cheek and a brief hug. "I have set up all of your rooms.

You have towels on your beds. You will tell me if you need anything more, yes?"

"Yes."

"Good. Now, here are your tickets for all of your activities. You'll go to the ecological station tomorrow morning very early." Alice groaned. Marta continued, undeterred. "You can go tubing and ziplining today. Ziplining first, I think. I told them to have a truck here an hour after the first bus arrived. I'll let you get settled."

"Thank you," we chorused. All of us trudged to our respective rooms. Alice and I put on our hiking boots. We always brought jackets, because the cloud forest was pretty cold in the morning. However, hiking heated you up pretty fast when you were slowly going up a mountain.

"I'm going to rest." Alice lay on her bed to get every second of sleep that she could before going out.

I had snacks, and I brought them to the treehouse. "Hey, guys. Is anybody hungry?"

Fitz and Jade were in the same state as Alice. Catie was reading. "Oh, I'll take some Oreos."

I gave her my Oreos. "Anybody else?"

"No," Fitz moaned feebly. "Early."

I sat on Catie's bed and ate some Oreos with her. I checked my watch. Fifteen more minutes to go.

"Catie, do you still have your waterproof camera? It might be fun to use while tubing, as long as you have the strap on your wrist."

"Yeah! That's a great idea." Catie knelt on the floor by her backpack. She stopped. "It's not a good idea of ziplining, but I'll definitely take it along when we go tubing."

"Yeah, perfect."

We had enough time to go out and do something, and I wasn't going to stay in the treehouse while Fitz and Jade were half asleep. "Do you want to go to the store next door? It'll take less than 10 minutes. We might as well pick some stuff up."

"Yeah, let's go." Catie took out her wallet. We headed to the convenience store next to Casa de Celia, and we bought crackers, Kinder Bueno, and Pringles. I took the Pringles, and Catie took the crackers and Kinder Bueno back to the treehouse.

"Alice, come on." I started jumping on her bed.

"Stop it, Jeff." She moaned. "I'll rip your balls off."

"Aliiice," I said. "Alice! I don't even have balls."

One eye opened. "I'll rip your ovaries off?"

"One, I don't think that's the same thing. Two, we need to go. Three, that wasn't a threat. It was a question."

"Fine. Fine." Alice rolled out of bed. "But it's on you."

"Ok. Let's go out to wait for the truck."

When we went outside, Fitz, Jade, and Catie were already climbing into the truck bed. We were the last ones. The drivers sitting in the cab of the truck were twins. They were tall and handsome, with the cheekbones of male models. They were also surprisingly pale. In Ecuador, most people were some degree of mestizo, with a little indigenous blood and a little Spanish blood. As a result, most Ecuadorians had a light perma-tan for which New Jersey housewives would kill. Maybe they were German. There were plenty of those in Ecuador.

"All in?" called the driver. He had a sexy accent, light, but it was definitely there.

"Yes," I called back.

"Vamonos."

The truck revved to life. We bumped down the road. In the United States, seatbelt laws outlawed riding in the back of truck beds. It was surprisingly comfortable. It wasn't unlike sitting in an open-backed limo, if limos had wheel covers that dug into your back.

It took less than 10 minutes to get to the ziplining place.

They unhooked the back of the

truck bed, and all of us climbed down. I was the shortest, but I'd learned to compensate for my height a long time ago. I was no Kacy Catanzaro from *American Ninja Warrior,* but I could handle a world that was just 1% too big for me.

The twins were standing at the side of the truck, staring at me and breathing hard.

"What?" I put a hand to my hair. It felt like it was fine in my braid.

The driver shook himself. "Nothing. I am Victor Abreu. It is a pleasure." He gave me a double-cheek kiss, the kind that Europeans did and Ecuadorians didn't. It looked like I was right about him being German.

"I'm Gabriella."

"I am Alonso." The other twin bowed to me, and he moved in, too. I was expecting a cheek kiss like Victor's, but he nuzzled my ear and smelled me, instead.

"You are delicious," he whispered into my ear. He kissed my neck. It was subtle enough that the four others wouldn't catch it. My knees felt loose. His hair smelled divine.

Victor was already walking up to get everybody's gear on. We had helmets. Alonso put my harness on me, touching me gently everywhere on my body. "I need to make sure it's safe." He tugged on every part of the harness, from the part near my breasts to the part next to my ass. With my body warmed up, it felt like foreplay. I blushed at the thought. Maybe German Ecuadorians were just really playful?

"Let's go." Victor pulled Alonso

forward in an very effective cock block. They looked at each other, with some secret twin communication passing between them. Alonso lead the pack, while Victor stayed in the back.

"I'm sorry about that. Alonso is very aggressive."

"I noticed. He seems like a nice guy."

Victor snorted. "I am the nice guy. He is my opposite, my twin."

I shrugged.

"We both want you, but he is much more obvious about it."

"Excuse me?" Maybe it was weird that Alonso would kiss me on my neck the first time that we met, but Victor was really bold in his own way.

"Could you not tell? We both had an incredible reaction the first time that we saw you. We each want to make you ours."

"I'm not a possession."

"No, you are a woman. Tell me, Gabriella, what is your last name?"

"Peres."

"Hmm, yes. Tell me, what is it that you want most in the world? If a genie could come down and give you your heart's desire, what would it be?"

Victor seemed overly familiar, but I thought about it.

"I'd want to be happy."

Victor nodded. "That is a good answer."

Was it? I felt like it was ambiguous. When I was in fourth grade, we'd talked about careers.

Someone in my class asked me about it.

What do you want to be when you grow up?

Happy.

That's not a real answer.

Victor didn't seem to think that it was a stupid answer to his question, though, and I was grateful for that.

"Come. We must hurry to catch up with the others." He pulled on my hand and started to run up the path.

The zipline course had 13 lines, and it started really high up, since zipping always went down.

"Let's do the crazy stuff!" Catie was saying as we caught up to the rest of the group. "I want to do Superman."

"Yes, you can do Superman. There are only two of us, though, so only two out of the five of you can do Superman on any line," Victor told her.

"I want to go first," Catie said.

"Good. I will take you." He climbed up the steps with her. He hooked her up to the zip line from the back of her harness, and he got on, too. All of the zipline instructors always wore special gloves on the lines. Fitz, Jade, and Alice were helped by Alonso.

"Do you want to do Superman?"

"Sure." He hooked me up. He put my legs behind him. I could feel his giant erection pressing into the juncture of my thighs.

He pushed us off, and we were flying above the top of the cloud forest. Everything was still misty, but I could see thousands of beautiful orchids at the tops of the trees below me. I was getting wet from feel him press into me, even though we were both fully clothed. The trip was incredibly short.

Victor helped unhook us. Alonso said softly, "Did you like that?"

"I think it's the best trip I've ever been on. I wish I could fly like that all the time."

Victor shook his head, and he took the group down to the next line. We followed that pattern on all of the rest of the lines, with Victor taking one of the other girls and then Alonso taking me at the end. By the end of it, my cheeks were flushed, and I was wetter than the cloud forest. I imagined that it wasn't that comfortable to have an erection for this long, but it was turning me on a lot.

There was a psychology study once with the idea of arousal and exhilaration. They made guys walk across a terrifying bridge, and they counted the ones who asked the research assistant for her number. The control group did something that wouldn't raise your heart rate, and almost none of them asked for her number. The majority of the bridge group. Yeah, I was incredibly turned on, but I didn't trust my body's instincts to make decisions for me when it came to boys. I avoided them for a reason. I'd seen my mom get involved with way too many men, and she'd neglect me when she was seeing someone new. I'd been too busy working and studying to ever have a boyfriend in high school and college, anyway.

I wasn't very experienced firsthand with boys, but I'd seen enough hanky panky that I knew it wasn't worth it. My friends always went through the cycle of meeting a cute guy, hooking up with him, and then breaking up with him for some reason. Sometimes it was as stupid as a tweet. Sometimes they cheated. I wasn't ready to be with a boy without a commitment. I'd done fine by myself for most of my life, and I had no intention of letting some guy turn me into a crying mess.

Alonso was changing my ideas, though. I'd watch my friends hook up with random frat boys for one night, the kind that never called. I saw the attraction now, though. Alonso was the sexiest guy I'd ever met, and it didn't hurt that he had an identical twin that could match him. I got the impression that in the contest between Alonso and Victor, Alonso had pulled ahead by a lot.

As they walked all of us back to the truck, Alonso trailed to the back so he could talk to me.

"Hey, do you like to have fun?"

I eyed him warily. "What kind of fun?"

"There's a club in Mindo called Tatumbe. Our friends all go there, drink a little, have a good time. You should bring your friends."

"We're going tubing today, and we woke up pretty early this morning."

"I'll make it worth your while," he promised.

"We'll see."

"We'll be there starting around 10."

"Ok."

"Do you want to sit in the cab with us?"

"No, I'd rather be in the truck bed."

"Oye," he called. "Does anybody want to ride with Alonso inside of the truck?"

"Me!" Catie climbed in. Alonso

lifted me effortlessly by my waist into the truck bed, then he climbed in after me. I'm not a small girl.

"You act like that was nothing."

"It wasn't. You are the perfect size." He wedged himself against me and the gate of the truck bed. His body was so hard, and he smelled so good. I could feel myself getting wetter by the second.

We couldn't talk in the truck bed, so he put his hand between my legs from underneath. My legs were together, but it didn't stop him. He felt my muscles clench on his fingers, and he smiled at me. Nobody else noticed. I stifled a moan with his firm, slow strokes. I was blushing. What if someone noticed? It felt too good to stop him, though.

All too soon, or just in time, we got

back to Casa de Celia. He let down the truck bed and helped me out, as well as all of the other girls in a show of gallantry.

"Tonight." It was a promise and a command.

"We'll see." I walked back to my room, and I could feel his gaze on my back.

EVENING

We had a blast going tubing, no matter how short I was. The water was moderately cold, but I didn't care. It was fun just to go out with my girls in bathing suits and float down a river.

Afterward, we agreed to meet up at 8 for dinner. All of us hit the showers, and we met in the treehouse at 8 smelling fresh as daisies instead of disgusting river water.

We went to El Quetzal for dinner. We ordered. While we were waiting, Catie went to walk around the restaurant. She came back with a pamphlet.

"Hey, guys. They have a chocolate factory tour. Do you want to go?"

That actually sounded fun. "I don't know. Do we have time?"

"Well, they do a morning and afternoon tour. Do you think that we could do it after ziplining tomorrow? It's at 4.

"Ok, if we feel like it tomorrow, we'll go. I promise."

Catie's lower lip stuck out. "Ok." She sat down next to Fitz.

We ordered our food and settled in. Fitz was talking to Catie and Jade about how boring literature class was, while Alice and I were having our own private conversation.

"So, those guys…"

I blushed. "I know, right?"

"They're twins! Get'em girl."

I sighed. "I don't know. It's too much to handle. And I'm only here for the weekend."

"You deserve to let loose. This isn't like hooking up with someone in Quito or back home. Mindo is basically another world."

"I think you're right." I probably was listening for what I wanted to hear, but she was right. Mindo could be my Vegas. "I guess we should go to the bar."

Alice bumped my shoulder with hers. "That's my girl."

With a speed uncharacteristic of Ecuadorian service, we got our food almost immediately. I ate my chicken breast with papas doradas. It was weird that they didn't debone chicken breasts in Ecuador, but like everything else, I got used to it. It was nice and salty, and the potatoes definitely hit the spot.

At the end, we gorged on fantastic chocolate brownies made with the chocolate from their chocolate factories. The texture was really dense, and the five of us shared two. It was the perfect amount. When we were done, I sat back in my chair.

"Do you guys want to go out?" I tried not to sound too hopeful.

"Let's go," said Jade.

"The guide was telling me earlier that the best bar in town is Tatumbe."

"Let's go there!"

I'd looked it up in my guidebook of Mindo, although honestly a circuit of the town would've shown us. When we got there, I knew we could not have missed it. It was the only place in town that had loud music coming out of it. It was dark inside. In Mindo, there weren't that many bars, and this was probably the most happening one.

All of us showed our university ID to the bouncer, and he let us in. We staked out a table in the back with our jackets on it. Fitz hung back, while the rest of us started dancing on the dance floor. It wasn't packed with bodies, but most Ecuadorians danced salsa, which took space. If you weren't careful on the dance floor, you'd get bodychecked by someone doing some fancy footwork.

They were playing the newest Enrique Iglesias, and all of us were having a blast. It was as if we'd woken up late after a refreshing night of sleep. Catie was an excellent dancer; she'd been taking ballet since she was three, and she was the best of us. Alice and I made it up as I went, and Jade had this incredible innate rhythm that made all of her movements seem effortless.

Mid-song, I felt hands creep on my hips. "Hey," he said in my ear.

I whirled around. "Alonso."

"Are you enjoying yourself?"

"Very much. Where are your friends?"

"They, ah, couldn't make it. But I brought Victor." Victor was heading our way with cold beers in hand. He had three.

He bent down to shout in my ear. "Do you want one?"

What the hell. It was my Vegas. "Sure!" I shouted back.

Alonso rolled his cold beer bottle on my arm, and I shivered. "Do you want to go somewhere more private?"

Vegas, I told myself. "Hey guys, don't worry about me, ok? I'm good." I waved to them. Victor and Alonso parted the sea of bodies to take me outside. I just followed in their wake. Outside of the club, I could actually hear again. The three of us still had our beers in our hands.

"I've been thinking about what you said to me earlier today."

"Oh yeah? What was that?"

"You said that you wanted to be happy. Did you mean that?"

"Yes, I did."

"If I could promise you that you'd be happy for every day of the rest of your life, would you come with me?"

He startled a laugh out of me. "That sounds a lot like a marriage proposal."

He shrugged. "Answer me."

"I mean, it's hypothetical, right?"

"Sure." He watched me carefully.

"Sure. It's what I want most in life. The pursuit of happiness is a fundamental American right for a reason, you know."

Alonso broke in. "Do you want your beer? You haven't touched it."

I raised my beer bottle, and I turned around to face the two of them.

"To happiness." They raised their bottles, too, and the glass made little clink sounds as I hit both of their bottles. I drank my first sip. The coldness of the beer felt good, and it slid down my throat pretty easily. The beer felt kind of sweet. I kept walking, and they kept pace with me.

"What's in this? It tastes like honey."

Alonso scratched his ear. "It's, uh, homebrew."

"You mean the bar microbrews?" He hesitated for a second, then he nodded. "That's pretty cool. Doesn't the elevation make that hard?"

"I don't know."

"Oh, well, ok." It wasn't that important. "Where are we going?"

"We're going to our house." Victor drank another sip of his beer. "We have better drinks than Tatumbe, and it will be easier for all of us to talk."

In a minute, we were there. Mindo was the size of a postage stamp. Victor unlocked the door, and he let me go inside first. Inside, everything was coated in shiny stuff.

"Wow!" I was practically blinded by

the bling in the room. "It looks like everything is made out of gold. Is this like the gold leaf in Iglesia de la Compañía?"

Victor took a long breath in. "Something like that. Would you care to take a seat?" There was a pretty couch with gold fleur-de-lis on a cream background. I sat down, and my beer rested on my knee.

"So, what do you want to talk about?"

"I want to talk about your perfect body, your scent, your eyes, your hair, your nose, the curve of your lip, the taste of your skin..." Alonso was coming on pretty strong, but I'd never heard prettier words spoken to me. Ever.

I smiled. "We barely know each other."

"We know each other enough. Would you mate us?"

"Do you mean have sex with you?"

"Yes, mating includes sex."

My gaze bounced between the two of them. Alonso had his hair tousled, and he was leaning back on his chair. Victor had perfect posture, and his hair was gelled perfectly. Both of them could have featured on the cover of a magazine. *Vegas.*

"Yes."

COUCH, BED, AND SHOWER

Alonso was on top of me almost before I got to the end of the word. He took my hands in his big ones and pinned them to the back of the couch. He gently bit my neck before parting my lips with his tongue and kissing me deeply.

Victor wanted to get in on this action, too. I could feel Alonso being pushed to one side, as Victor put his huge hand inside of my top. He pinched my nipple, and I jerked. His other hand went to unbutton my jeans, and he had to use two hands to get the button open. I was really self conscious about the pudge that formed when I sat down, and I tried to back away, even though there was no room. Lifting my shirt, Victor went down to kiss my stomach.

"You're so feminine." He unzipped my jeans, and he pulled down my panties and my jeans in one fell swoop. Alonso bit my ear, and I arched. He let go of my hands, and I put them in his hair, controlling the angle of the kiss. He didn't let me do that for long. He pushed my hip so that I was laying on the couch. He pulled off my top, and he began biting my breasts.

Victor bit the inside of my thigh,

and I involuntarily jerked my hips towards him. "Patience, Gabriella." He stroked my clit lightly with his thumb. He was driving me wild, and we hadn't gotten to the main event yet. He put his tongue inside of me, and I bucked hard against his face. He pinned my hips to the couch more forcefully, and he began tongue fucking me in earnest. With each lick, I felt myself go higher.

Alonso was tired of foreplay. "Let's go to the bedroom." He slid his arms under me, and he carried me to a bedroom. Like the living room, this room was also gold themed.

I barely had time to notice that, though, because Alonso was taking off his clothes. His dick was massive. He had the build of a swimmer, with broad shoulders and tight abs.

"It's so sexy when you look at me like that, love."

Victor was taking off his clothes, too. They were identical in almost every way, except Alonso had a spiraling dragon tattooed on his left hip.

"Cool tattoo," I said, as the two of them advanced towards me on the bed.

"You like dragons?"

"I love dragons. I used to dream about becoming one. Dragons are so powerful and wealthy. I guess that's just in stories, though." It was a strange conversation to be having when naked, but they had a way of making me open up.

"Well, this dragon wants to fuck you now." Alonso pushed me on my back, put a pillow under my hips, and pulled my legs over his shoulders. He bumped my dripping hole with the head of his cock.

"Mate me."

"Yes. Please. Please."

He pushed it into me. It hurt for a second, then it felt amazing. He thrust and retreated, and it felt better than anything ever had.

Victor wasn't going to miss out on the fun. He went to the top of the bed, and he straddled my face while putting his hands on the wall above me.

"Suck me."

I'd never done this before, but I was willing to try. From the way that he moaned when I licked my way around the crown of his dick, he liked it. He began to thrust rhythmically into my mouth in counterpoint with Alonso's thrusts inside of me. I could taste his precum, and it was delicious and salty. I could feel the muscles in his thighs tense, and I knew he was about to come. In the second before he shot into my mouth, he pulled out.

"No. This first time, it is inside of you. Alonso, pull out."

Alonso growled, but he pulled out. Victor laid on his back. His hand was on his dick, and his hard cock was pointing straight up.

"Mate me."

I straddled his body, and I took his cock slowly into me. I was so wet that it slid in with no resistance. I hesitated when I had all of him inside of me, to get used to the sensations at this angle.

"Kiss me." I leaned down to kiss him. He put his tongue in my mouth, and we fought for dominance of the kiss.

Alonso came up behind me, and he

pushed me so that my entire torso was flat on Victor's. He started gathering wetness from my thighs and pushing it past my taint to my asshole. I tensed up and stopped kissing Victor. I put my hands and was about to push up.

"Shh," he soothed. "I won't hurt you."

I relaxed, and I settled back into making out with Victor. He was a much gentler kisser than Alonso. Victor was, in so many ways, more of a gentleman than Alonso. Alonso took what he wanted. Victor did, too, but I knew he'd always ask for something new if he could.

Alonso pushed his thumb inside of my ass. It was covered in my juices, but my sphincter was tight. Nothing had ever been up there before. He pushed just a little in and out, getting deeper with each thrust from Victor.

The scent of sex was in the air. The rhythm with Victor got harder and faster, and I stopped Frenching him in order not to bite his tongue with the intensity of my impending orgasm. Victor put his big hands on my hips, and he pulled me hard into him, getting even deeper. I cried out as I came, ecstasy bursting inside of me. I panted hard. I rested on Victor's chest, limp with the force of my orgasm.

Both of them were still hard.

"Do you trust me?" Alonso's accent was so sexy.

"Yeah."

He pulled apart my ass cheeks, and he pushed something that was way bigger than his thumb towards my ass.

"Relax. It'll be better. I just have to get past the beginning."

Victor wasn't thrusting now. He was stationary. Slowly, Alonso pushed his dick, still lubricated with my juices, inside of my ass. It burned, yes, but it felt incredible. With two cocks inside of me, I felt like I should be bursting. However, it was perfect. They were perfect.

Alonso pulled back, and he thrust into me again. I threw my head back and gasped for breath. He took a handful of my hair, and he kept me arched like that.

"I like the way you feel." My glutes were pressed on him. He roughly pushed into me. Victor set up the rhythm again, too. They coordinated pushing into me. Each would retreat when the other advanced. I was helpless, stuck between them, sweat on all of our skin.

Alonso picked up the pace, and Victor responded accordingly. I put my face into Victor's neck, and he swept a soothing hand down my back. Alonso slapped my ass hard.

"I'm so close."

Alonso pulled my hair even harder as I felt the first of his hot seed spill into my ass. I fluttered around him in my own orgasm. With a grunt, Victor began to release, too, inside of my womb.

Alonso rolled off of me. In the aftermath, this didn't seem like Vegas.

"I'm not on the pill."

"We didn't think you were."

"You didn't use condoms."

"We're clean, and you're a virgin."

"I was a virgin. But I'm not worried

about sexually transmitted diseases. What if I get pregnant?"

"If you get pregnant, it would be a tremendous gift." Victor was so serious, even though we were naked in bed. All of us were covered in various amounts of bodily fluids.

"I have a life, you know. Getting pregnant would really ruin going to college and holding down a job. I can barely afford to provide for myself, let alone a baby."

"Money's not a problem for us. We'd support you in whatever you chose to do. We could buy a college for you."

I snorted. "Be real." I looked into his eyes.

Victor looked dead serious. "I am."

I got off of him. My pussy and ass felt so empty compared to before.

"You're being weird." I looked around for my clothes, then I remembered that my clothes hadn't made it into the bedroom.

I looked down at myself and sighed. I didn't want to get jizz and blood all over my clothes. I didn't have that many in Ecuador, so I needed to clean up. I went to their bathroom.

I ran the sink, but Alonso's hand went to turn the faucet off.

"Hey!"

"Shower." He picked me up and put me in the shower. They had cross jets at shoulder height that sprayed my body with water. Both of them were fully erect again. Victor and Alonso got in with me. Victor's back was against the wall, and Alonso was at my front. Alonso pulled me into his arms, and my legs were around him. He pushed into me. Even though I felt sore, it felt so good that I didn't protest as he set up a rhythm.

Victor kissed the center of the back of my neck, and he snaked his hand around to play with my clit as his brother thrust into me. He took his other hand to part my ass cheeks. I was still plenty wet inside, and he shoved into me, without the waiting that Alonso had done. It burned, but I knew how good it would feel once he got all the way in.

The spray of the water was all around us. Alonso was pushing me harder and harder into Victor. I could feel their dicks swelling inside of me, and they burst, shooting seed into me.

In the aftermath, Alonso set me on my feet. He kissed the top of my head. "Thank you."

Victor was soaping up his hands. "Come here." He lathered the soap on my back, on my neck, on my breasts. His hand went down the center of my body, and he slid his slick, soapy hand into me.

"We need to clean you up." He pulled it from my clit to my back door. He kissed my shoulder.

"Close your eyes." Alonso was pouring shampoo on his hand, and he started to wash my hair. It felt so good and intimate. He captured my mouth again. This time, it wasn't foreplay. It was just kissing, with the three of us in the shower.

When they had cleaned every inch of my body, they turned off the water jets. Alonso picked me up again to set carefully on their marble bathroom countertop. He took a towel, and he dried me off, paying special attention to my breasts, which still bore the marks of being bitten by him. He was completely unconcerned with his own nudity, and his body was a masterpiece, especially with the dragon tattoo on his hip. He saw me looking at it.

"Would you like to be a dragon? It just takes a bite."

I didn't know what he was playing at, but it felt good when he bit me.

"Yes."

Victor came to my other side. Both of them bent down to bite my shoulders, and I felt my body get aroused again, even after all my orgasms. It shot pain and pleasure inside of me, racing neck and neck for dominance. They bit hard enough to just barely break the skin, and I could feel their tongues soothe the places their teeth had pierced.

"Come, let's get you clothes." Victor wrapped a towel around me, and he picked me up to carry to the bedroom. "Do you like blue or black?"

"Blue, I guess." Victor shifted so my weight was on one hand. It was still effortless for him. He reached for a blue robe inside of the closet. He carried me to the bed, and he let me sit down.

"Here." He helped me put the robe on. I tied the sash. I could see myself in the closet mirror, though, and I still had bite marks on my cleavage from Alonso.

"There's something we need to talk about."

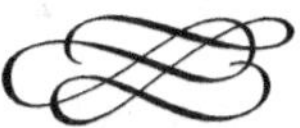

I laid back, feeling content. "Yeah, what's that?" I put my hands behind my head and crossed my legs.

"You're a dragon now."

That got my attention in a hurry. I sat up. "What?"

"You consented to being Changed."

"I did no such thing."

"You agreed to mate us, and you agreed to becoming a dragon."

This guy was clearly unbalanced. "Okay…" I needed to bolt so I could get my clothes.

Victor put his hand on my arm. "No, look." His arm changed so that it was covered in purple scales.

I started to hyperventilate. Alonso closed the bedroom door. "Stay and hear us out."

I didn't really have a choice. "Ok." The second I could manage it, I was bolting out of this madhouse.

"You're our mate for life. We'll cherish you with every breath we take." Victor used such pretty words.

"We'll mate every day." Alonso sometimes did not.

Victor watched me carefully. "You know how I asked about your last name?"

"Yes."

"It was to check that our first instinct was correct. We knew it from the moment that we saw you that you could be our mate."

"How?"

"Your smell and your abundant curves." Alonso trailed a hand from my boobs to my ass.

"Not very many women could become a dragon. For a lot of them, their body would reject the Change. For you, though, drinking our blood did not make you immediately throw up."

"I did *not* drink your blood."

"You did, though. It was in the beer."

"How could you slip it in my beer without asking me first?"

"We did. We asked you if you would mate us if we could make you happy, and you said yes. You are ours for eternity."

"You'll never have to worry about money again. We have long lifespans."

"What about my real life? It's not like I can hide out in the Andes forever. People will notice that I'm gone."

"That's easy." Victor flicked his fingers, and a perfect copy of me appeared. "We'll send a simulacrum in your place."

"People will be able to tell it's not me."

"No one will be able to tell it's not you. You haven't noticed the simulacrum in your group."

"What? Who?" Please let it be Catie.

"It's the one you call Alice. She mated two dragons in the Galapagos recently."

I gaped at them. "What? No. She's my best friend. I would know."

"The simulacrum was made by someone right by her. She's the queen of the Brood, too, so that doesn't hurt. The magic is very strong. All simulacra are formulated to act exactly as the human would act."

"Alice is a dragon queen?" This talk was so bizarre.

"Yes. Would you like to speak with her? We can form a telepathic link using any mirror." Victor raised his hand and said a few short, emphatic words. The mirror on the closet showed me Alice.

I walked up to it. "Hello?"

She looked up. "Oh my gosh! Gab!" She pressed her hands on her side of the mirror. "Gab! I wish I could hug you right now."

"What are you doing in the mirror?"

"You know, don't you? Victor and Alonso called in for permission earlier today to find a mate. I got interested when they told me her name was Gabriella."

I felt tears prick my eyes. "How could you leave me and never say a word?"

"I couldn't. But my simulacrum was there to keep you company."

"It's not the same as you."

"It is, though. It's the life that I would've lived if I hadn't chosen to be queen. I see everything that happens to my simulacrum in dreams. It's hard to differentiate between dreams and reality. I don't know if I'm living a normal life and dreaming about being a queen, or living as a queen and dreaming about real life. Maybe this is all happening as we both dream from our beds in our apartments."

"I can assure you that I am awake."

She smiled. "You would say that. Anyway, do you want to join the Brood?"

"The Brood?"

"It's our extended family. The purple dragons have South America, and I lead them."

"If you're real, then I think I'm already a dragon."

"Try. Try to change your hand into a claw."

I looked down at my hands. Neither of them turned into a claw.

"I don't think I'm a dragon."

Alice rolled her eyes. "You aren't really trying. Imagine that your hand is a claw. What shape is it? It's purple with scales. You have talons."

I looked down and imagined my hand as she described it. My hand changed.

"Holy shit!"

"You'll get used to it, I promise."

"Don't you miss me? Don't you miss our real life? Is being a dragon queen totally normal to you now?"

Alice sighed. "Yes, I've settled into being a dragon queen. Of course I miss you. I've missed you every day that I've been here. But I can't go back. My simulacrum is living my life. I have another one here now, doing important things for a lot of people. That's what you want most, isn't it?"

First, happiness. Now, impact. But both answers were true. "Yes."

"You can be the Viceroy of the Andes, if you want."

"You can do that?"

"I'm the queen. I can do anything." She smiled like a cat who got the cream. "You can make an impact. You can help thousands upon thousands of dragons. And once you learn to fly, you can go anywhere in the world that you want to be."

It sounded pretty tempting. "I don't know if I want to live a double life like you, though. It sounds really disorienting to bounce between two realities."

"You could always let your simulacrum disappear, you know. You'd just have to 'die' in a plausible way, that's all."

Alonso cut in on our girl talk. "We could do it on a zipline."

Alice nodded, encouraging him to continue with her hand. "Go on."

"It's simple. Her carabiner fails, and she falls into the cloud forest. No one will ever be able to find her body. There won't even be one. We'll just take back the magic in the simulacrum."

"How does that sound?" Alice turned to me. I was clad in a robe, and I felt self-conscious.

"Will you guys really make sure that I'm happy for every day of the rest of my life?" I needed to feel sure of that before I could make the decision to leave my old life behind.

"We promise." They both had their hands over their hearts.

"Dragon oaths are sacred. If they ever break their promises, their blood will boil in their veins. There is no cure."

I nodded. "Ok. I'm in."

"You guys need to get busy then. I'll talk to you soon, Gab." Alice waved goodbye, and the mirror went back to being a mirror.

"What do we need to do?"

"First, we need to take the pin out of a carabiner so that it looks like it's whole but isn't. I think that we need to do this on the first line, because the carabiner won't hold for long."

"Ok."

"I can take you first in front of your friends, and you'll be on your own when you drop."

"Why do you guys even work anyway, if you have so much money and can actually fly?"

"I like interacting with people.

Mindo is a quiet place. There's not much variety here."

"Why do you live here at all, then?"

"Can you keep a secret?"

"Yes, of course."

"This is where some of the Incan gold is."

"You mean the Incan gold that Atahualpa told his people not to send to the conquistadors?"

"Yes, that Incan gold."

Shit. I guessed that explained the decor of their home.

"Can't you move it?"

"It's in the mountain."

"Can't you take it out?"

"You don't understand. It's *in* the mountain. It can't be taken out without unstablizing the mountain."

"Oh. Ok."

"We should send you back. Your

friends will worry if you are gone all night. I'll walk you back to Casa de Celia."

Victor walked me back to the main room, and I picked up my clothes and got dressed. He pulled me into him with an arm around my shoulders in the cold night, and I huddled into his body heat. He felt like a furnace, which was wonderful in the Andes at night.

It took a few minutes to get to the hostel. We were quiet on the way over, each thinking our own thoughts. Outside of the hostel, he bent to kiss me. "Until tomorrow."

"Tomorrow," I promised.

ZIPLINE

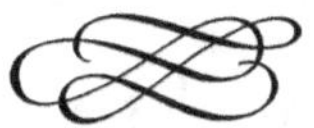

Alice's simulacrum was waiting up for me when I got back. "How was it? Was it great?"

"It was great." I could never look at this simulacrum the same again. "I need to rest now." It was past midnight, and we were going to the ecological station in the morning before dawn.

Bright and early, my cell phone

alarm went off. I made Alice's simulacrum get out of bed, and I brushed my teeth.

A truck came to get us, and it took us to the ecological reserve. A German ecologist came out to greet us.

She walked us through the forest, identifying all the plants by name.

"Do you notice that every flower is some shade of red or pink?"

We looked around. Everything looked like it belonged in the room of a 5-year-old princess. "Yeah."

"That's because hummingbirds, which are major pollinators in the cloud forest, can see infrared. The more red you are, the greater chance you have of reproduction. There are thousands of hummingbirds. We've recorded more than 200 species just on sight."

We walked through the cloud forest as she explained everything to us, and we ended up back at the reserve at the end of the trail, which looped.

"I will give you hierba luisa tea. I think you will find it good." She lead us to a porch. In front of the porch was a bunch of birdfeeders. There were dozens of hummingbirds there, and none of them were alike. She poured all of us a hot cup of tea, and we sat and watched the hummingbirds flit around crazily, eating a bit here and there.

When all of us had finished our tea, she took us back to where we'd met the truck. It was idling there, and it took us back to Casa de Celia.

When we got back to Casa de Celia, Victor was waiting in a truck.

This was it. This was the last I'd see of my old life. I had packed everything into my backpack the night before. Alonso would make sure that it ended up in their home. They were sending someone to my home in Quito to gather my belongings before the news of my "death" hit my host parents. I knew my mom wouldn't care if my stuff went missing, but my host parents probably would notice if I died and suddenly all of my stuff disappeared after the funeral.

The guy in the passenger seat was no one I'd seen before. All of us girls climbed in the back, and we took the short ride to the ziplining place. The new guy, who introduced himself as Jorge, lead the front, while Victor hung back with me.

"I'm going to make you invisible and send your simulacrum now. Don't panic. I'll teach you how to do it yourself later."

I nodded. He said a few words. I looked down at myself. I waved my hand in front of my face. I couldn't see it.

"You can still make noise, so you need to be careful. I just thought you'd like to see this yourself."

"Ok."

Victor hurried to catch up with the others, and my simulacrum hurried, too. He outfitted her with all the gear and the faulty carabiner. He pushed his way to the front of the line, and he set her up on the line. I held my breath as she zoomed out to the middle, and she screamed as she fell down. Fitz,

Catie, and Jade were screaming too. Alice simulacrum's face was shocked. Jorge sat down hard on the ground.

"Mierda."

Gabriella Peres was gone.

EPILOGUE

After I faked my death, all of my stuff was put in Victor and Alonso's house. Alice made me the Viceroy of the Andes, and my life settled into a comfortable rhythm of governing the Andean region.

I was sad that I'd missed out on all the trips to the rainforest and the tropical coast that my group would take, but my new life was worth every bit of the sacrifice I'd made.

Alice breathed deeply. Castor had just saved her life. Pollux was his mirror image, but she'd bet that he'd do the same for her, no matter what the cost.

"I don't want different mates. I want you both."

Pollux slid her body down, and he captured her mouth with his. He tasted like the best wine she'd ever had, an incredibly expensive vintage. He tasted better, and kissing him felt like warm wine slipping down her throat. Castor was behind her, and she could feel a gigantic erection pressing into her back. With both of them pressing on her, it was a little hard to breathe. It was a thousand percent worth it, though.

Castor was pulling down everything. Her swimsuit was gone. She could feel his bare skin on hers. Pollux was suddenly naked, too. Maybe clothing was easy for dragons to get off by magic.

Think later. Feel now.

Suddenly, Castor pulled her off her feet and detached her from Pollux. He carried her back into the cave, like a bride over the threshold. Pollux settled behind her, letting Castor take the lead this time. Castor thrust his tongue into her willing mouth. She loved it when Castor was dominant. He tasted like the best chocolate ever invented. Pollux was pulling apart her cheeks. He began to eat her out from behind, which no one had ever done to her before. His tongue was expert, pushing just the way she liked it. She groaned in ecstasy.

Castor took it as a cue to bring things to the next level. He moved so that she had to take his dick into her mouth, and his head was between her thighs. His hand and mouth went to her clit, and she fell over the edge, just like that. When the fireworks stopped exploding behind her eyeballs, she opened her eyes to see that Castor was on top of her, biting her neck and breasts and leaving a necklace of bite marks at her throat and cleavage. She was flat on her back; Pollux was somewhere else.

The mystery of where Pollux went was not too long, however. Castor turned her so that they were both laying on their sides, and Pollux took back his position behind her.

"Do you trust me?" he asked, nuzzling her ear.

"Yes." Though she hadn't known them long, she knew that she could trust them with her life.

He pulled on her cheeks again, only this time he was heading for another hole. She tensed up and squeaked. Castor went back to rubbing her clit.

"Shh, my heart. It will be good. You will see."

She could feel Pollux rubbing something into her ass. She tried to relax, but she'd never had anything up there before. She was a virgin at the front and back doors.

"I've never…"

"It's ok. Just trust me. Trust us."

She could feel him work his thumb into her. It felt so big, and it burned.

"Shh. It's just the tip. It gets better once I get inside."

She was breathing hard now, stimulated by the pleasure Castor was giving her and the painful pleasure that Pollux offered. Pollux had worked his entire thumb in, and though it still burned and she felt incredibly stretched, she felt a little bit good.

"Good?"

She breathed in. "Good."

Castor took that as his cue to push his cock into her wet slit. She grunted at the sudden insertion. There'd been no warning at all. She could feel the burn as she stretched all the way around his enormous girth. The pain elevated her pleasure, and this was the most intense sex she'd ever had in her life. She looked up at his face, and she saw how pleasurable it was for him. Castor kept a slow and steady rhythm, and she went higher and higher, moaning in time with his thrusts. Her whole body was shaking with the force of pleasure. She was so full, but somehow she needed more.

Pollux took his thumb out, and he pressed something much bigger to her back door. It was slicked up with whatever he'd used to lubricate her hole, and he worked it into her bit by bit. She knew to expect the burn now, and it was distracting to have Castor plunging into her at the same time. Her eyes were closed, and everything happened in a blind world where she could smell and feel everything. The scent of the dragons, the feeling of Castor's bites, the pull and burn in both holes, the solid presence of Pollux at her back…everything was overwhelming. She felt herself spiraling towards the sun, and this time Castor and Pollux were flying with her.

Pollux and Castor set up a faster, more demanding rhythm now. She felt their rougher thrusts pulling her apart.

Get it now: Galapagos

CRAVING THE ALPHA

Craving the Alpha

CHASED BY THE DRAGONS

Galapagos

Mindo

Puyo

Canoa

OUTFOXING THE ALPHA

Part 1

Part 2

Part 3

BEARFIELD

A Slice of Honeybear Pie